Sam and Ruby's Olympic Adventure

by

Tony Bradman

and

the young people of Hackney

Illustrated by Martin Remphry

For Hayden – at last!

Thank you to everyone who helped with the book, including:

Ademosu
Agnieszka
Jennifer Akinola
Sakib Ali
Murat Apat
Michael Ayomide
Bailey
Haleemah Bakht
Amani Banemeck
Rolene Basuama
Jordan Collymore
Tariq Creary
Rebecca Dale
Zaynab Daudo
Dilan
Arran Graham
Lauren Hands
Hatice

Troy Henderson-Ryan
Shaquille Hinkson
Michael Hogarth
James Howell
Kaitlin Joseph
Kartal
Kaur
Khan
Luke Langford
Ryan Marr
Yumun Mehboob
Monica
Martina Neunie
Sasha Njoku
Oluwatoyin
Elsie Daisy O'Rourke
Kehinde Oyebola
Taiwo Oyebola

Aaron Pinnock
Przygodzka
Rubel Rahman
Roche
Rajan Sagar
Sahan
Salli
Milo Seaman
Seetal
Satpal Singh
Jamie Skinner
Aiden Smith
Aiysha Thomas
Gokhan Tuna
Luke Vidal
Lorenzo Webster
Wong
Zilan

First published in 2012 in Great Britain by
Barrington Stoke Ltd
18 Walker St, Edinburgh, EH3 7LP

www.barringtonstoke.co.uk

Copyright © 2012 Tony Bradman
Illustrations © Martin Remphry

ISBN: 978-1-78112-084-2

Printed in China by Leo

Contents

Chapter 1
The Head's Office ... Again!

Sam and Ruby waited outside the Head's office. Sam sat and tapped away at the keys on his laptop while Ruby topped up her lip gloss, then leaned against the wall and started to play with her phone.

The door opened. The Head – his name was Mr Clark – looked out at them and gave a deep sigh. "Well, well, who do we have here?" he said. "Could it be The Dreadful Duo? The Terrible Twosome? The Horrors of

Hackney? What a surprise ... I don't think. You'd better come in, I suppose."

Sam and Ruby moved forward at the same time and got stuck in the door.

"Oww, what a rubbish driver you are!" yelled Ruby. "Your wheelchair's on my toe!"

"It's not my fault!" snapped Sam. "It's your big bum that's got us stuck!"

They struggled for a few seconds more, then burst in. Mr Clark was sitting behind his desk. There were two chairs in front of it. Sam crashed into one and knocked it over. Ruby sat down on the other, crossed her arms and leaned back.

"Now let me see, what have you two been up to?" said Mr Clark. He put on his glasses and peered at a sheet of paper on his desk. "My, my, a long list of crimes this week so far, and it's only Tuesday. I'll start with you,

Sam. The list says you've not been listening in class, you've been cheeky, and I understand you hacked into the school website on Monday."

"I was only trying to help," said Sam. "It needed a tidy up."

"That's very kind of you, Sam," said Mr Clark. "But I'm not sure that swapping all the teachers' photos for photos of animals makes it much better. Mrs Wilson is rather upset that you swapped her picture for a picture of a hippo."

"She should be pleased," said Ruby. "The hippo is better looking!"

"You got that right!" laughed Sam, and they fist-bumped each other.

Mr Clark shook his head. "As for you, Ruby," he said, "I don't even know where to start. You're cheeky too, and the teachers say you're too busy thinking about your hair and make-up to listen in class. They say you're always playing with that phone of yours as well, even though you know you should have it turned off in school."

"I wish I could turn off the teachers sometimes," said Ruby.

"What a great idea!" said Sam. "I could fit them with a switch ..."

Sam and Ruby laughed and fist-bumped each other again. But Mr Clark didn't laugh. He looked grim, and at last Sam and Ruby fell silent. Mr Clark gave another sigh, an even sadder one than before.

"This can't go on, you know," he said. "We've tried everything with you two, but you just keep getting into trouble again and again. I don't understand it ... you're both very clever! But you won't get anywhere in life if you carry on like this."

"What are you going to do, then?" said Ruby, and blew a bubble with her gum.

"Are you going to exclude us?" asked Sam.

"Oh no," said Mr Clark. "That would be far too easy." All of a sudden he smiled an evil smile. "I'll give you both one last chance to show me just how clever and well behaved you can be. I want you to do a project on the

Olympics and present it to the whole school at assembly this Friday."

"Oh no, do we have to?" moaned Ruby. "I *hate* all that Olympics stuff ... I wish they'd never given the Olympics to London. It's just so ... *lame*."

"Totally," agreed Sam. "I hate the Olympics too."

"Sorry, kids," said Mr Clark. "You don't have any choice. And if I don't think your project is good enough, I won't let you go on the big trip to Islands of Adventure with the rest of your year. Got that?"

"But ... but ... that's not fair!" shouted Ruby. "You can't be serious! We've paid our money!"

"Oh, I am very serious, Ruby," said Mr Clark. "Off you go, and shut the door on your way out."

Chapter 2
An Old Movie

"We might as well kill ourselves now," said Ruby. She and Sam were hiding behind the stage in the school hall. "There is no *way* I'm going to do a project on the Olympics. He can shove it up – "

Sam broke in. "Be like that, then," he said. "But I'm not giving up the chance of a trip to Islands of Adventure. I've been looking forward to it all term. You saw the website – it's got the best rides in the world!"

"I know, I know," said Ruby. "But we can't do it. We've only got two days to work on the project, and there's no way Mr Clark will let us get away with stuff copied and pasted off the net."

"Yeah, we'll have to do a lot better than that," said Sam. "Hang on, this reminds me of something ..." He tapped at his laptop. "Have you heard of an old film called *Bill and Ted's Excellent Adventure*?"

Ruby shook her head.

"My dad showed me it," said Sam. "It's about two teenagers who get in trouble at school. They have to do a history project, and they go back in time to do it. They collect famous people from the past with a time machine made from a phone box and bring them back to their school for assembly."

"You mean like *Dr Who*?" said Ruby. "I don't like *Dr Who*."

"I love *Dr Who*," said Sam. "I'm sure we could do the same thing."

"Yeah, right," said Ruby. "In your dreams."

"No, listen to me," said Sam. "I bet you some nutcase has written about how to build a time machine somewhere on the net. We just have to find out where."

"Go on then, geek," said Ruby. "I suppose we've got nothing to lose."

Ruby kept watch while Sam hacked into all sorts of websites on his laptop. NASA, the CIA, MI5 (and MI6, 7, 8 and 9) ... until he found just the thing they needed.

"Got it," he said, with a grin. "Check it out, Ruby!"

"*Time Travel for Dummies*," Ruby read over his shoulder. "*Build your own Time*

Machine with stuff you have at home already. Sounds mental."

"I like mental," said Sam. "I'll make a start as soon as I get home. But we need to think about how we're going to present what we find out. Bill and Ted took the people they collected into school. But we can't bring back everyone who's ever been in the Olympics, can we?"

"Not unless you build a very big time machine," said Ruby. She looked at her phone and grinned. "I know, why don't we make a film? I could use my phone, it's got an ace camera."

"Wicked!" said Sam. "I love it when a plan starts to come together ..."

That night, Sam worked hard in his bedroom. The police in Hackney got lots of phonecalls about funny noises, bright flashes and loud bangs from his block of flats. But the next morning in class Sam grinned at Ruby and gave her a thumbs up.

Later, after school, Sam showed Ruby the machine.

"Check it out," he said, and whipped off the sheet he'd put over the machine. "I used my spare wheelchair as the base. I've built my laptop into it, and added a step for you to stand on at the back."

"Wicked!" said Ruby. "So what are we waiting for?"

"Nothing," said Sam. "Climb on ... and let's go!"

Chapter 3
It All Begins ...

Sam took his seat in the time machine and Ruby stood behind him. He tapped at his keyboard and the chair's engines began to hum. Soon it was spinning faster and faster and blue lines of power crackled from the metal.

"Wait a second," said Ruby. "Where are we going to go?"

"Don't stress," said Sam. "I've programmed the laptop to take us on a tour of all the Olympics from the start up to the present day. But you'd better hold on tight – it could be a bumpy ride …"

Just then there was a loud *BANG!* and several flashes. The chair took off into the air like a rocket. It belched out flames, and around them the sky changed from dark to light, over and over again.

"This is *wicked!*" yelled Sam. "Are you OK, Ruby?"

"I think so!" screamed Ruby. "When will it stop?"

"NOW!" shouted Sam, just before they landed with a *BUMP!* in a grove of trees beside a field. There were mountains in the distance, and the sun shone down from a clear blue sky. It was very hot. A huge statue of a god with a lightning bolt in his hand stood over a line of white buildings.

"I'd better check exactly where we are ..." said Sam, and started to tap at his laptop.

"Forget it," said Ruby. "Any idiot could see this is Ancient Greece."

"Nice one, Ruby," said Sam. "We'd better find someone to talk to."

"How can we do that?" asked Ruby. "We don't speak Ancient Greek."

"Chill," said Sam. "I thought a translation program might come in handy, so I built one into the machine. We can talk to anyone we meet."

"Wicked," said Ruby. "Look, there's a boy with some sheep ..."

The sheep boy was called Alexios, and after he came round from fainting in shock, he turned out to be dead nice. He told them they had landed in a holy place. The statue was of a god called Zeus.

Ruby got her phone out and filmed Alexios and the statue.

"This is Olympia," Alexios told them. "People from all over Greece come here to compete with each other every four years."

"Ah," Sam said. "That's why it's called the Olympics."

Then Alexios told them how all the cities in Ancient Greece were like little countries and they fought each other all the time.

"But war is banned when the Olympic Games are on," he said.

"Have you ever taken part?' asked Sam.

"No," said Alexios. "You won't catch me running any races naked!"

"Naked?" said Ruby. "OMG. I don't think I'll film that."

"I think we've got enough, anyway," said Sam. "The laptop is feeding us more info as well ..." He started to read from the screen. "The first Greek Olympics were probably held in 776 BC ... the word *athlete* comes from the

Greek word *athlon*, which means 'a prize'. OK, that's plenty. I think it's time to go!"

"Thanks, Alexios!" said Ruby. They waved goodbye and soon they were travelling through the years again, with flames belching out behind them.

They stopped in Olympia every few years, and saw the games get bigger and bigger. But then things began to change. The Romans invaded Greece. By 400 AD, there were no more games, and grass grew over the race track.

Sam and Ruby talked to another shepherd, who was also called Alexios – it seemed to be a popular name. He told them the Romans had banned the games.

"Maybe they had better things to do," said Ruby. "But it seems a shame."

"Well, someone must have started the games up again," said Sam. But not for a very long time. The laptop says our next stop is in 1894 ...'

Chapter 4
The Baron with the Briefcase

As Sam and Ruby raced back to the future they saw empires rise and fall, wars start and end, and famine, disaster and amazing inventions change the world. At last they arrived in 1894. The time machine crashed down in a quiet street near a large building.

"Where are we?" asked Ruby, looking around. "This could be any city in the world."

"We're in Paris," Sam said. "The laptop says there's going to be a meeting in that building today – one that will be very important for the Olympics. And here comes someone who can tell us all about it!"

Sam pointed at a man who was walking towards them. He had a big moustache and he had on a posh suit and a bowler hat. In his hand he had a briefcase that looked as if it was about to explode, and it was clear he was in a big hurry.

"Him?" said Ruby, surprised. "He looks as if he's on his way to work."

"Well, that's what the laptop says," said Sam. "His name is Baron de Coubertin, and he's the man who got the Olympics going again."

"We'd better film an interview with him, then," said Ruby. "Excuse me, Mr ... er ... Baron?"

"Can't stop!" said the Baron, with a shake of his head. "I'm late, very late!"

"We wanted to ask you about the Olympics," said Ruby.

The Baron stopped in his tracks and stared into the sky, his eyes all misty. "Ah, the Olympic Games!" he said. "They are my life's work, my dream!"

"Can you tell us why that is?" asked Ruby, like a reporter on TV. "What got you interested in sport in the first place?"

The Baron turned out to be very happy to tell them all about himself.

"I grew up in a rich family here in France," he said, "and I have liked sport for as long as I can remember. Then I went to England and found out about the Olympic Games."

"London?" said Sam. "But the games were in Ancient Greece!"

"Yes, yes," said the Baron, "but in England I saw your fantastic public schools."

"Fantastic?" said Sam. "They're just full of posh kids."

"Ah, but they all do sport," said the Baron. "In French schools when I was growing up we didn't do any sport at all! And that's not good. A healthy mind in a healthy body, that's what I say. I loved your rugby, your cricket ..."

"I don't get it," said Ruby. "What's all that got to do with the Olympics?"

"Well, the children I met in your public schools all learned Latin and Greek," said the Baron. "So they knew about the Olympics in Ancient Greece."

The Baron told them about a group of people in Wenlock, Shropshire, who had put on a kind of mini Olympic games in 1850. Later on in the 1800s the Greek government itself had started to talk about getting the games going again in Athens.

"Why did you get involved?" asked Ruby. "You're French!"

"I think all countries should take part in the Games," said the Baron. "I think that holding the games every four years might lead to the end of war. Countries who have played sport together won't want to fight each other any more, will they?"

"Sorry to tell you the bad news, Baron," said Sam. "But I don't think that idea worked out very ..."

"Er ... that's great, Baron, thanks," said Ruby. She shoved Sam to shut him up and then turned back to the Baron. "Can you tell us what your meeting today is about? Who will be there?"

"People are coming from all over the world," said the Baron. "We are going to set up an International Olympics Committee. Once we've got that up and running we can start sorting out the first games. Anyway, I must dash!"

The Baron hurried off towards the doors of the large building. Lots of other people were going the same way and soon he was lost in the crowd.

"He seemed nice, and very keen," said Ruby. "It's a shame his idea about stopping war didn't work out." She looked at Sam. "Where to now?'

"Back to Greece, it looks like," said Sam and pressed a button on his laptop ...

Chapter 5
A Force for Good ... and Evil

It was just a short hop for the time machine to Athens in 1896. Sam and Ruby landed inside a brand new stadium where some people were racing on the track. A crowd was watching, but it was just a small one.

"Is this it?" said Ruby. "The first modern Olympics? I'm not impressed."

"I suppose everything starts small," said Sam. "And maybe this isn't as small as we think. What's that noise?"

Sam and Ruby both turned around and looked up ... and up ... and up. The tallest man they had ever seen was standing behind them. His legs were the size of tree trunks and he was waving a British flag. There were lots of other people behind him. They all had flags from different countries.

"Look, there's the French flag!" said Sam. "And a German one!" He started to count. "Wow, Ruby. There are 14 different flags here. That means 14 different countries." He smiled at Ruby. "I wish we had a flag," he said. "They look really cool!"

"Saddo," said Ruby. "I wonder how many athletes are here. There have to be more somewhere."

"Indeed there are," said a deep voice. Ruby looked up in surprise. The tall man was talking to her.

"There are 241 athletes taking part in the Olympics," the man said. "I'm one of them."

"Good luck in your race, mate," said Sam. "You look like you can run really fast."

The man laughed. "Thank you. If I win I'll come and show you my medal!"

"Gold!" said Ruby. "Ace."

The man looked at Ruby like she was mad. "The winners' medals are silver, my dear lady," he said, and walked off.

"Did you hear that?" Ruby said to Sam. "They give the winners silver medals, not gold! That's just cheap, that's what that is."

Sam and Ruby watched the races for a bit. It was a bit like sports day at school.

"I think we should move on, see how things turned out later," said Ruby.

So that's what they did. They said goodbye to their new friends and got onto the time machine again. They ended up in Stockholm, in Sweden, in the year 1912.

"It's all starting to look pretty much like the modern games," said Sam. He nodded at the flag flying over the stadium with its five linked rings. "That's the symbol of the games, one ring for each of the continents in the world."

"And, look!" said Ruby. "They've got the right medals now. Gold for first, silver for second, bronze for third. Proper bling!"

"Oh look," said Sam, "there's the Baron giving out medals. Hey, Baron! Remember us? Good to see you again!"

The Baron looked at them, puzzled. But then he smiled and waved back. "Hello, my friends," he shouted. "These are the winners of the poetry competition! I won the first one with my poem *Ode to Sport*!"

"They have a competition for poetry?" said Ruby. "That's even more lame than competitions for sport."

"It's mental," said Sam.

"Just like the Baron," said Ruby, and they both laughed.

But there was not much reason to laugh when they moved on next. The sky over Europe seemed to grow dark. The First World War broke out in 1914, and there were no Games in 1916.

"So much for the Baron's plans to end war," said Ruby. "Countries still went to war even though they played sport together. Poor Baron."

After the war Sam and Ruby saw the first Winter Games, in France in 1924. There were people ski-ing and everything!

"This looks good," said Ruby. "I'd like a go on a sledge. We never get any snow in London."

"I don't see anyone in wheelchairs, though," said Sam. "We've not seen anyone in a wheelchair since we started. Apart from me."

"Stop moaning," said Ruby. "Or I'll push you down the hill, wheelchair or not!"

Sam took off before Ruby had a chance to try it.

"Where should we land next?" he shouted.

"What's that down there?" Ruby asked. "There's a funny symbol on those flags?"

Sam looked grim. "It's a swastika," he said. "The symbol of the Nazis. We must be in Berlin, 1936."

"Oh no!" Ruby said. "We better go back! You mean Adolf Hitler and his troops, don't you? I know about them. They hated Jews and black people, and disabled people. Anyone who was different. They started the Second World War and killed millions of people."

"I think we'll be safe if we stay near the time machine," Sam said. "I think they won't want anything to happen to spoil the games."

"Hang on, there's a race starting," said Ruby. "I want to film this."

One of the American runners was black. His name was Jesse Owens, and the Nazis booed him when he ran.

At the other end of the track there was a man with a little moustache, sitting in a box at the front of the crowd. Ruby gasped. "That's Adolf Hitler!" she said.

"He thought the Berlin Olympics would show the world that white people were the best," Sam said.

When Ruby heard that, she cheered for Jesse Owens as hard as she could. He won. And he went on to win three more gold medals.

"Three cheers for Jesse!" yelled Ruby. "I bet Hitler's well angry!"

"I don't think he's enjoying the Olympics much," said Sam. "The German team has just lost to India at Hockey, so all the white people aren't winning!"

"That's great," said Ruby. "But can we go? I don't feel safe here. Let's go somewhere else."

"Your wish is my command," said Sam, and they whizzed off once more.

Chapter 6
It's Only Fair ...

"I don't think this is any safer!" yelled
Sam in a panic. He flung the time machine to
one side just as a British plane flew past,
chasing a Nazi bomber through the air. "I
think we're going through the Second World
War years!" he said. "This looks like the Blitz
to me – when the Nazis bombed London!"

"I think you're right," said Ruby. "Hey, I
can see Hackney down there! It's getting

hammered. There are bombs going off all over the place. I hope my house is OK."

It turned out that there were no Olympics in 1940 or 1944 because of the war. At last Sam and Ruby came into land again, in a stadium that looked a bit run down.

"Well, here we are back in London," said Sam. He grabbed a newspaper that was blowing past and looked at the date. "It's 1948," he said. "That's three years after the war. There must not have been much money left to fix things. Everything still looks a bit bashed about from the bombing."

"It's not just the buildings that are bashed about," said Ruby. "Check out those guys."

Sam looked where she pointed. A group of young men was watching the races. They all seemed happy, and they were enjoying the athletics – but they were all in wheelchairs. Sam and Ruby looked at each other and then went over to them. Ruby got out her phone.

"Hi," she said to the men. "Would you mind telling us a bit about yourselves? We can't help but see that you've all, er … well, been hurt in some way …"

"Oh yes, we've got a set of war wounds between us, haven't we, lads?" said one of the men. "We're all ex-soldiers hurt in the war. We met at a hospital called Stoke Mandeville. They tried to mend us there."

"It didn't work?" asked Ruby.

"No," said one of the men. "But at least they mended our heads!"

"Yes," said his friend beside him. "One of the doctors put on some sports events for us, to show us we could still do things. It was great. So then he said we should compete in the Olympics! It's only fair – why should it only be for people who can walk?"

"Those guys are cool!" said Ruby, as they watched the men line up for their race later on. "Imagine what they must have been through in the war. I'm so glad that Hitler and the Nazis were beaten. Are you happy now, Sam?"

"I will be when I see them race," said Sam. And he wasn't disappointed. He and Ruby whooped and cheered for their new friends. They were faster in their wheelchairs than Ruby would be on her legs!

They jumped forward again, to 1952 in Helsinki, Finland, and Melbourne, Australia in 1956, and saw more wheelchair events for people who had been hurt in the war. By the 1960 games in Rome, anyone in a wheelchair could take part in the games, whether they had been in a war or not. Sam left Ruby watching a race while he went even further ahead.

"It's amazing," he said, when he came back. "I knew there was something called The Paralympics, but I didn't realise it was that good! Did you know that by the 1988 Games in South Korea, thousands of great disabled athletes were competing? Some of them were in wheelchairs and some weren't. There were all kinds of people doing sport."

"Good," said Ruby. "You should have a go too, Sam."

"Do you think so?" said Sam, surprised. "Well, maybe I will ..."

Sam told Ruby that the name Paralympics had nothing to do with being "paralysed". The name came from the Greek word "para", and it meant that the Paralympics ran at the same time as the Olympics. The Paralympics were here to stay.

"Well that's great," said Ruby. "But I've found out about another problem. One of the crowd here told me that some countries have started to pay athletes, so they can afford not to have jobs and train all the time."

"Isn't that normal?" Sam asked.

"Not in these times," Ruby said. "They say the Baron and the others who set up the Olympics thought no one should be paid. And it's not fair if some athletes are paid and some aren't. I've got a feeling that it's going to lead to some big arguments ..."

Ruby was right. But there was even bigger trouble to come, as they soon found out.

Chapter 7
Bullets and Bombs

By now the time machine was pretty much flying itself, so Sam and Ruby could relax and focus on the Games. They whizzed on to Tokyo, Japan in 1964 and then Mexico City in 1968.

"Listen," said Ruby. "Can you hear the music?"

It was the American National Anthem, being played at a special event for the winners of the Games.

Sam was quiet. He was trying to see what was going on down in the stadium.

"Can you see those two black athletes?" he asked Ruby. "They're standing really still and their heads are down. And look, they're both wearing black socks and no shoes."

Ruby stared. Sam was right. Then she saw that the two black men had one hand each in the air, with a black glove on.

"It looks like a protest," Ruby said. "In the 60s black people in America weren't treated as equals."

"Oh, right," said Sam. "We got told about that in school."

"I think those protesters are being sent home," Ruby said. "That's terrible."

They tried to stop the time machine, but it kept going and didn't stop until 1972, when the Games were in Munich, West Germany.

"I wish we'd stayed longer in 1968," said Ruby. "I wanted to talk to those black athletes."

"Yeah, I know," said Sam. "But hang on a second – er, why is it all so … quiet here?"

The stadium in Munich was empty, and no events were taking place. Sam and Ruby went to the Olympic Village, where the athletes stayed while the games were on. They weren't allowed in – there were police with guns and news crews everywhere.

"This looks bad," said Ruby. "Let's ask that reporter what's going on."

They found out that it was all to do with problems in the Middle East. A group from Palestine was holding the team from Israel hostage. Two of the team had been killed. Now the kidnappers wanted a helicopter so they could leave.

"We have to see what happened," Ruby said. "Get the time machine to show us, Sam. This is awful!"

What happened next was even more awful. The police tried to free the hostages when the helicopter came, but nine of the team were killed, along with all the kidnappers, and one policeman as well.

"I don't think I want to carry on now," said Ruby. She had tears in her eyes. "I mean, how could they have kept the Olympics going after that? Those people just used the Games to try to get their message to all the people watching!"

"I suppose if you gave up every time something bad happened then nobody would do anything," said Sam.

"I suppose so," said Ruby.

"Look how big the Games have got," Sam said. "It's the biggest sporting event in the world! Just think how proud the Baron would be. Don't you want to see what happened next, Ruby?"

"Oh, all right," Ruby said. "I just hope we don't see any more fighting."

Their next stop was Montreal, Canada in 1976. The Games there were a great success, and nothing bad happened.

"There you go, Ruby," said Sam. "Sorted!"

But there was more trouble in 1980. The Games were in Moscow in Russia. At that time Russia was part of a country called the Soviet Union. The Soviet Union had invaded Afghanistan, and as a protest the USA and many other countries would not send teams to Moscow, even though the Games still went ahead.

"That was a bit cheeky of the USA, wasn't it?" said Ruby. "Haven't they invaded lots of places? They invaded Afghanistan themselves after 9/11."

The Russians got their own back, though. When Sam and Ruby landed at the next Olympics, in Los Angeles in 1984, there was no Russian team.

"What are these grown-ups like?" said Ruby. "They're worse than kids!"

They moved on in the time machine, still filming, still finding out stuff for their project. They went to North Korea in 1988, Barcelona in 1992, and then Atlanta in the USA in 1996 – where someone let off a bomb.

"I don't believe it!" said Ruby. "More people killed!"

"It's not all bad," said Sam as they whizzed past Sydney in Australia in 2000. "Look at all those people down there! They're having fun, and they're only watching the opening event. Wait till you see Beijing, China in 2008. I watched some of that – it was wicked!"

"I think it's too big," said Ruby. "It must cost so much money. It must be too much for poor countries. And if they can't afford to pay their athletes the same as rich countries,

rich countries have a better chance of
winning."

"So do people who take drugs," said Sam.
"Cheats."

They had found out that some athletes
had taken drugs to make them perform
better. This meant that some had had their
medals taken away.

Ruby sighed. "I think it's time we went
home and did some editing," she said.

Chapter 8
A Great Story

The whole school sat in the dark hall, waiting to see the film Sam and Ruby had made. Sam had linked his laptop to a big screen so everyone could see. Ruby did a short speech first. She was very nervous.

"I hope Mr Clark likes it," she whispered to Sam. Mr Clark was sitting at the side of the hall with all the other teachers. "We'll be in hot water if he doesn't."

"It's too late now to worry about it," whispered Sam. "Right, here goes ..."

He tapped a key on his laptop and the film began. They had spent ages doing the editing, but they had got everything in – the ancient Greeks, the Baron, the early Olympics with all those athletes in old-fashioned outfits. They put in something from each Games, including the Winter Games and the Paralympics. They also put in the bad things – the Nazis booing Jesse Owens, the terrible tragedy at Munich in 1972, the bombing in Atlanta, and athletes being banned for taking drugs.

But Sam had been right when he had told Ruby there were lots of good things to show. They showed all the great athletes they had seen – runners Jesse Owens, Emil Zatopek, Usain Bolt and Kipchoge Keino, swimmers Mark Spitz and Michael Phelps, gymnasts Olga Korbut and Nadia Comaneci. Then there

were all the great British Olympic heroes …
Seb Coe, Daley Thompson, Kelly Holmes,
Steve Redgrave, Chris Hoy, Ellie Simmonds.

Then there were shots of the big parties
in London when the International Olympic
Committee awarded the 2012 Games to
London, and the Olympic Park being built.
And at the end Sam and Ruby had put
themselves on screen talking to each other.

"So what do you reckon then, Ruby?" said Sam, up on the big screen. "Olympics – good or bad?"

"They've been both," said Ruby. "But I tell you one thing, Sam – they've never been boring. It's a great story, and I can't wait for 2012 to begin …"

The screen faded to black, and there was silence in the hall. Then everyone started clapping and cheering, and Sam and Ruby took a bow.

"Not bad," said Mr Clark, smiling. "I knew you could do it. And now you can go on the trip to Islands of Adventure. Thank goodness – it would have been boring for the teachers with no Sam and Ruby to keep them on their toes. So, what's next for the Demonic Duo?"

"I think I might start training for the Paralympics," said Sam.

"And I'm going to start looking for a job as a TV reporter," said Ruby.

"You will remember me when you're famous, won't you?" said Mr Clark.

"No," said Ruby. "I will not." She winked and Mr Clark smiled.

Sam and Ruby fist-bumped each other and ran all the way to the school gates.